Teeny Tiny

retold by Jill Bennett
pictures by Tomie dePaola

G. P. Putnam's Sons
New York

For Colin   J B

For Laura and Jeffrey Bastron   T D E P

First American edition, 1986.
Text copyright © 1985 by Jill Bennett.
Illustrations copyright © 1985 by Tomie dePaola.
All rights reserved. Originated and published
in Great Britain by Oxford University Press, 1985.
Printed in Hong Kong by South China Printing Co.
Book design by Ellen S. Levine
Library of Congress Cataloging-in-Publication Data
Bennett, Jill. Teeny Tiny.
Summary: Retells the tale of the teeny-tiny woman
who finds a teeny-tiny bone in a churchyard and puts
it away in her cupboard before she goes to sleep.
[1. Folklore—England] I. dePaola, Tomie. II. Title.
PZ8.1.B4143Te 1986 398.2′2′0942 [E] 85-12347
ISBN 0-399-21293-0
G. P. Putnam's Sons, 51 Madison Avenue,
New York, New York 10010
First impression

Once upon a time there was a
teeny tiny woman who lived
in a teeny tiny house
in a teeny tiny village.

One day this teeny tiny woman
put on her teeny tiny hat

and went out of her
teeny tiny house
to take a teeny tiny walk.

When the teeny tiny woman
had gone a teeny tiny way
she came to a teeny tiny gate.

So the teeny tiny woman
opened the teeny tiny gate
and went into a
teeny tiny churchyard.

In the teeny tiny churchyard
she saw a teeny tiny bone
on a teeny tiny grave
and the teeny tiny woman
said to her teeny tiny self,

"This teeny tiny bone
will make some
teeny tiny soup
for my teeny tiny supper."

And so the teeny tiny woman
took the teeny tiny bone
from the teeny tiny grave
and put it in her
teeny tiny pocket

and went back to
her teeny tiny house.

When the teeny tiny woman
got to her teeny tiny house
she was a teeny tiny bit tired.

So she went up her teeny tiny stairs

and put the teeny tiny bone
into her teeny tiny cupboard

and got into her
teeny tiny bed.

When the teeny tiny woman
had been asleep for
a teeny tiny while
she was awakened
by a teeny tiny voice
from the teeny tiny cupboard
which said,

'GIVE ME MY BONE!'

And the teeny tiny woman
was a teeny tiny bit frightened,

so she hid her teeny tiny head
under the teeny tiny bedclothes
and went to sleep again.

And when she had slept
a teeny tiny time
the teeny tiny voice
cried out again
from the teeny tiny cupboard
a teeny tiny bit louder,

'GIVE ME MY BONE!'

This made the teeny tiny woman
a teeny tiny bit more frightened,

so she hid her teeny tiny head
a teeny tiny bit further
under the teeny tiny bedclothes.

And when the teeny tiny woman
had been asleep again
for a teeny tiny time,
the teeny tiny voice
from the teeny tiny cupboard
said a teeny tiny bit louder,

'GIVE ME MY BONE!'

The teeny tiny woman
was a teeny tiny bit
more frightened,

but she popped her teeny tiny head
out of the teeny tiny bedclothes
and said in her loudest
teeny tiny voice,

'TAKE IT!'

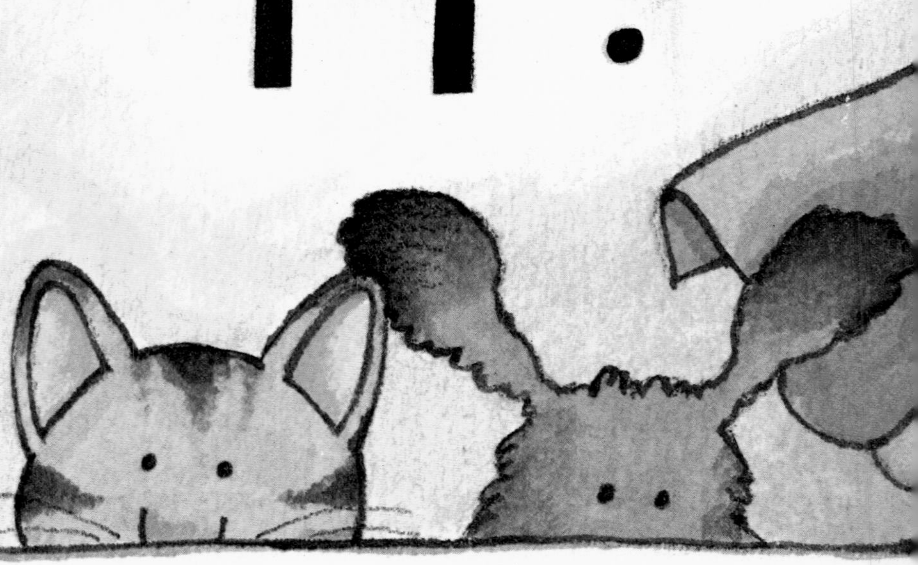

Convent of the Sacred Heart

1 East 91st Street

New York, N.Y. 10128